Hey Jack! Books

The Crazy Cousins
The Scary Solo
The Winning Goal
The Robot Blues
The Worry Monsters
The New Friend
The Circus Lesson
The Bumpy Ride
The Worst Sleepover

First American Edition 2013
Kane Miller, A Division of EDC Publishing

Text copyright © 2012 Sally Rippin
Illustration copyright © 2012 Stephanie Spartels
Logo and design copyright © 2012 Hardie Grant Egmont

First published in Australia in 2012 by Hardie Grant Egmont

For information contact:
Kane Miller, A Division of EDC Publishing
P.O. Box 470663
Tulsa, OK 74147-0663
www.kanemiller.com
www.edcpub.com
www.usbornebooksandmore.com

Library of Congress Control Number: 2012956112

Printed and bound in the United States of America
1 2 3 4 5 6 7 8 9 10
ISBN: 978-1-61067-185-9

Hey Jack!

The Worst Sleepover

By Sally Rippin

Illustrated by Stephanie Spartels

Kane Miller

A DIVISION OF EDC PUBLISHING

Can't stay still

Feels like jumping with excitement

Wiggly Mood

Chapter One

This is Jack. Today Jack
is in a wiggly mood.
He is wiggling and
jiggling so much he
can't keep still.

Tonight Jack is going to
his friend Jem's house.
Jack has never had
a sleepover at Jem's
before.
Jem has a Wii and a
PlayStation *and* a
computer in his room.
Jack and Jem are going
to play games *all night*.
Jack can't wait.

At last, it is time to go.
Jack's dad drives to
Jem's house. Jem opens
the front door.

"Hey, Jack," Jem grins.
"You're *finally* here!"

"Jem is *very* excited,"
says Jem's mom to Jack.

"Me too!" says Jack.

The two boys run into Jem's room.

"See you tomorrow!" Jack's dad calls.

Jem's room is very cool. First Jack and Jem race cars on the PlayStation. Next they play sports on the Wii. Then they go on the computer to build cities. It is lots of fun.

"Let's go outside and play soccer," says Jem after a while.

"Nah," says Jack.

"How about we build
a fort, then?" says Jem.

Jack shakes his head.
He is too busy playing
on the computer.

"Well, *I'm* going outside!"
Jem says crossly.
He **STOMPS** out of
the room.

Hmm, thinks Jack.

What's wrong with Jem?

He quickly finishes
his game. Then he goes
outside to look for Jem.

Jem is in the backyard.
He is kicking a soccer
ball against the fence.
Jack goes over to see
if Jem is OK.

But just then, Jem's mom
calls them for dinner.

Jem rushes past Jack without even looking at him. Jack follows him inside. He feels confused. Jem is acting very strangely!

Chapter Two

Jack and Jem sit up
at the table.

"I hope you like
spicy food, Jack?"
Jem's mom asks.

"Um, sure," says Jack.
He is too shy to
tell her he has never
tried spicy food before.

Jem's mom puts a big
dish on the table.

"Not curry again!"
Jem grumbles.

"Jem," says his mom
crossly. "You'll eat
what you are given."

Jem's mom puts some
rice on Jack's plate.
Phew! Jack thinks.
I like rice.

But then she spoons
curry over the rice.

14

Jack can see chicken,
carrots and potatoes
in the yellow sauce.
Jack doesn't like
carrots much. He feels
nervous.

Jack looks at Jem. He is
eating everything. Jack
pokes his fork into a
piece of chicken. He puts
it into his mouth.

Suddenly his mouth

starts to burn.

His eyes water.

16

"Oh dear," says Jem's mom. "Is the curry too hot for you, Jack?"

Jack swallows the chicken. Then he takes a big drink of water to try to cool his mouth. "Maybe a little bit," he says to Jem's mom in a squeaky voice.

17

Jem giggles.

Jack frowns. *Why is Jem laughing at me?* he thinks. His cheeks get red and **hot**.

"That's all right, Jack," she says. "You don't have to eat it. I don't know what I'm going to give you for dinner, though."

"I like rice," Jack says shyly.

"Can I just have rice, too?" Jem asks.

Jem's mom shakes her head. "Jack is our guest," she says. "He is allowed to eat what he wants. You need to finish your dinner as usual." She gives Jack a bowl of plain rice.

"Aw, that's not fair!" says Jem crossly.

"Sorry," whispers Jack
to Jem. But Jem
pretends not to hear.

Jem eats all his dinner
without looking at
Jack once.

Jack can't understand
why Jem is acting
so strangely.

"Would you boys like to watch a DVD before you go to bed?" asks Jem's mom. "I have to do some work."

"Yes, please!" says Jack.

"Whatever. I don't care," says Jem **grumpily**. He sits down on the couch next to Jack.

The two boys watch
a movie. The movie
is very funny, but Jem
doesn't laugh once.

Jack wishes he was back
at home. At least when
he watches a movie with
his mom and dad, they
laugh at the funny bits.

Jack feels a little bit
grumpy with Jem.

Jack had been
looking forward to
this sleepover for
a long time. It was
supposed to be the
best sleepover ever.
Instead it has turned
out to be the worst!

Chapter Three

After the movie
it is time for bed.
Jack and Jem change
into their pajamas
and brush their teeth.

Jem's mom comes
to say good night.

"Hope you boys are
having fun," she says.
"Don't stay up too late
talking, will you?"

Jack lies in the dark.
He wishes his mom and
dad were here to kiss
him good night.

28

Instead there is just grumpy old Jem who won't even talk to him.

Jack feels lonely.
He wonders if it is
too late to call his
mom and dad to
come and get him.

Just then, he hears
a noise. A sniffly, snuffly
sound. Jack realizes
Jem is crying!

"What's the matter?"
asks Jack.

30

Jem stops crying.

"Nothing," he says.

Now Jack feels **cross**.

"Why won't you
talk to me?" he says.

Jem sits up in bed.
He turns on his
bedside lamp.
"You are the boringest
friend ever!" he shouts.

"What?" yells Jack.

"No, I'm not. *You* are! You said we could play games all night and now you don't want to!"

Jack is so angry he feels like he might explode.

Suddenly Jem bursts out laughing.

33

"*What?*" says Jack.

"You look funny,"
Jem giggles.

34

"I've never seen you look that cross before. You look like an angry monkey."

Jack tries not to smile, but Jem's laughter makes his mouth **twitch**.

"Well, *you* look like a grumpy gorilla!" he says.

Jem laughs. "You should have seen your face when you tasted Mom's curry," he says. "You went all red like a baboon's bottom."

Jack frowns. "I haven't eaten spicy food before," he says. "It's not my fault!"

"Don't worry," Jem says kindly. "You have to get used to it. I've been eating curries since I was a baby!"

"Do you really think I'm a boring friend?" Jack asks.

"Of course not!" says Jem. "I just wanted you to come and play soccer, that's all."

"But you have so many cool video games," says Jack. "Don't you want to play with them?"

Jem shakes his head. "Not all the time.

Usually it's just me and Mom at home. I have to play video games by myself. It gets boring. And she never wants to play soccer. That's why I was so excited about you coming over. Finally, someone to play with!"

Jack feels bad.

He might not have

any video games, but

he always has someone

to play with – his dog,

Scraps, his best friend,

Billie, even his mom

and dad sometimes.

He was so **excited**

to play Jem's games

that he hadn't thought about what Jem might want to do.

"All right," says Jack. "Tomorrow it's your turn to decide what we play."

"Cool!" says Jem. "But don't you want to beat my high score on the computer first?"

"Nah," says Jack, smiling.
"I think I'd like to
beat you at soccer.
That sounds like
much more fun!"